House
Sparrow

American Crow

Downy
Woodpecker

Northern
(Baltimore)
Oriole

Two Blue Jays

Anne Rockwell
pictures by Megan Halsey

WALKER & COMPANY
NEW YORK

For

Nicholas, Julianna, Nigel, Christian —A. R.

For

my father and mother and the house they built for me at 25 Old Forge Drive —M. H.

First published in the United States of America in 2003 by Walker Publishing Company, Inc.

Published simultaneously in Canada by Fitzhenry and Whiteside, Markham, Ontario L3R 4T8

For information about permission to reproduce selections from this book, write to Permissions, Walker & Company, 435 Hudson Street, New York, New York 10014

Library of Congress Cataloging-in-Publication Data
available upon request
ISBN 0-8027-8840-8 (hardcover)
ISBN 0-8027-8841-6 (reinforced)

The illustrations for this book were created on colored artist's paper with acrylic, then individually cut out and glued in layers to create a three-dimensional piece of art.

Book design by Victoria Allen

Visit Walker & Company's Web site at www.walkerbooks.com

Printed in Hong Kong

2 4 6 8 10 9 7 5 3 1

Two blue jays sat on a branch of the big fir tree that grows right outside our classroom window.

One flew away, but the other stayed.

Soon the one that flew off came back with a seed in its beak.

The one that stayed opened its beak,

and the other fed it the seed.

“That bird’s very nice to share its food,” said Julianna.

“It has a reason for doing that,” said Miss Dana. “A good one. The blue jay that found the seed is a male.

The other is a female.
The male blue jay feeds the female
before they build a nest."

Both blue jays flew off.

When they came back, each bird was carrying a twig in its beak.

We watched as the two blue jays flew off and came back

and flew off and came back, again and again.

They were always carrying twigs to put on the branch of the tree.

We made a mark on our calendar that day, so we'd remember

when our two blue jays began to build their nest.

40
+29

When it was time to go home,
the twigs were starting
to look like a nest.
By the next morning,
one of the blue jays was sitting in it
while the other perched on a branch.
"Male and female blue jays look alike,"
Miss Dana said.
"But I think that's the female
sitting on the nest.
That's where she'll lay some eggs
that are inside of her."

The male blue jay flew off and came back with food.

The female opened its mouth, and the male fed it again.

They did that many times.

We made a list of what the male brought back in its beak.

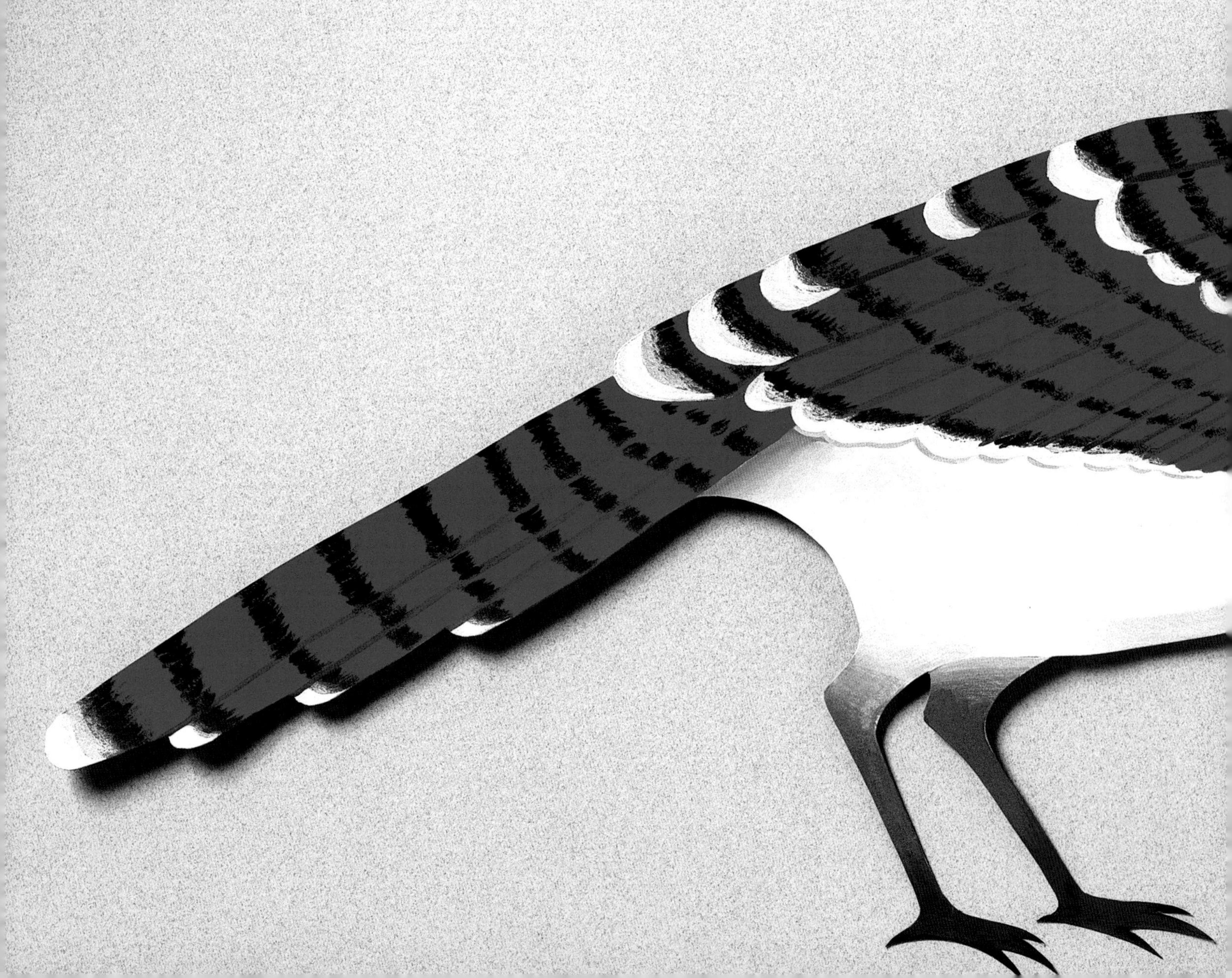

peanut
caterpillar
sunflower seed
grasshopper
earthworm
grape
acorn
piece of cookie?

Jay!
Jay!

When he wasn't searching for food,
the male perched on the branch,
looking around with black beady eyes.
When a cat came sneaking to the base of the tree,
the male blue jay flapped its wings
and cried out with a loud "Jay! Jay!"
It squawked so loud the cat ran away.

Lillie

One morning I came to school early.

I saw the female hop onto the edge of the nest.

Four brownish green and speckled eggs were in the nest!

They were smaller than chicken eggs.

I didn't get to look at them long,

since the female quickly hopped back into the nest.

Every day we looked out the window,
trying to see the eggs in the nest.
But we couldn't because the female
was always sitting there.
"The mother bird sits on the eggs
to keep them warm," Miss Dana said.
"Why?" I asked.
"Because baby blue jays are growing
inside those eggs," she said.
"Wow!" I said.

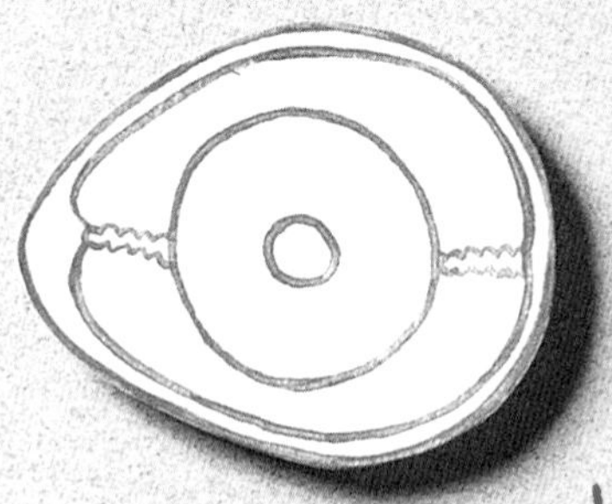

baby blue jay growing inside egg

Sixteen days have passed since our two blue jays built a nest.
Today the female hopped out of the nest and onto the branch.
We saw four baby birds inside the nest!
"I never saw anything so funny looking," said Abby.
She was right. They weren't cute and cuddly
like some baby animals are.
They had wide-open beaks and eyes that were closed.
Their grayish pink skin was loose and wrinkled.
Not one of the baby birds had a single feather.

When the male blue jay came back,
it fed one baby something so tiny we couldn't see what it was.
Then the female flew off with him
and came back and fed them, too.
Those baby blue jays kept their mouths wide open all day,
making little hungry squawks,
eating whatever their parents brought.

Every day those baby blue jays ate and ate
and grew and grew.
Their eyes opened into round black beads.
Downy feathers soon covered their skin.
They began to look more like the two big blue jays.

Three weeks later they were covered with feathers.

They were too big to fit in the nest.

The two big blue jays hopped and squawked

until the baby blue jays hopped onto the branch.

It was time for them to try to fly.

They didn't even need a single lesson.

They just spread their wings and flew down from the tree.

They flew pretty well, considering they'd never done it before.

The male didn't feed the female anymore.

The two big blue jays didn't feed the babies, either.

They didn't need to.

Now those baby blue jays could fly off to find insects

and seeds and leftover peanuts,

along with bits of this and that.

Soon the nest was just an empty clump of old twigs.
The wind blew it off the branch one night.
We brought it inside the next day
and kept it on the windowsill.
It made us remember our two blue jays
and the eggs the female laid
in the nest they built in the big fir tree.
Now whenever I see a blue jay or hear it squawking
"Jay! Jay! Jay!"
I always wonder if it's one of ours.

Blue

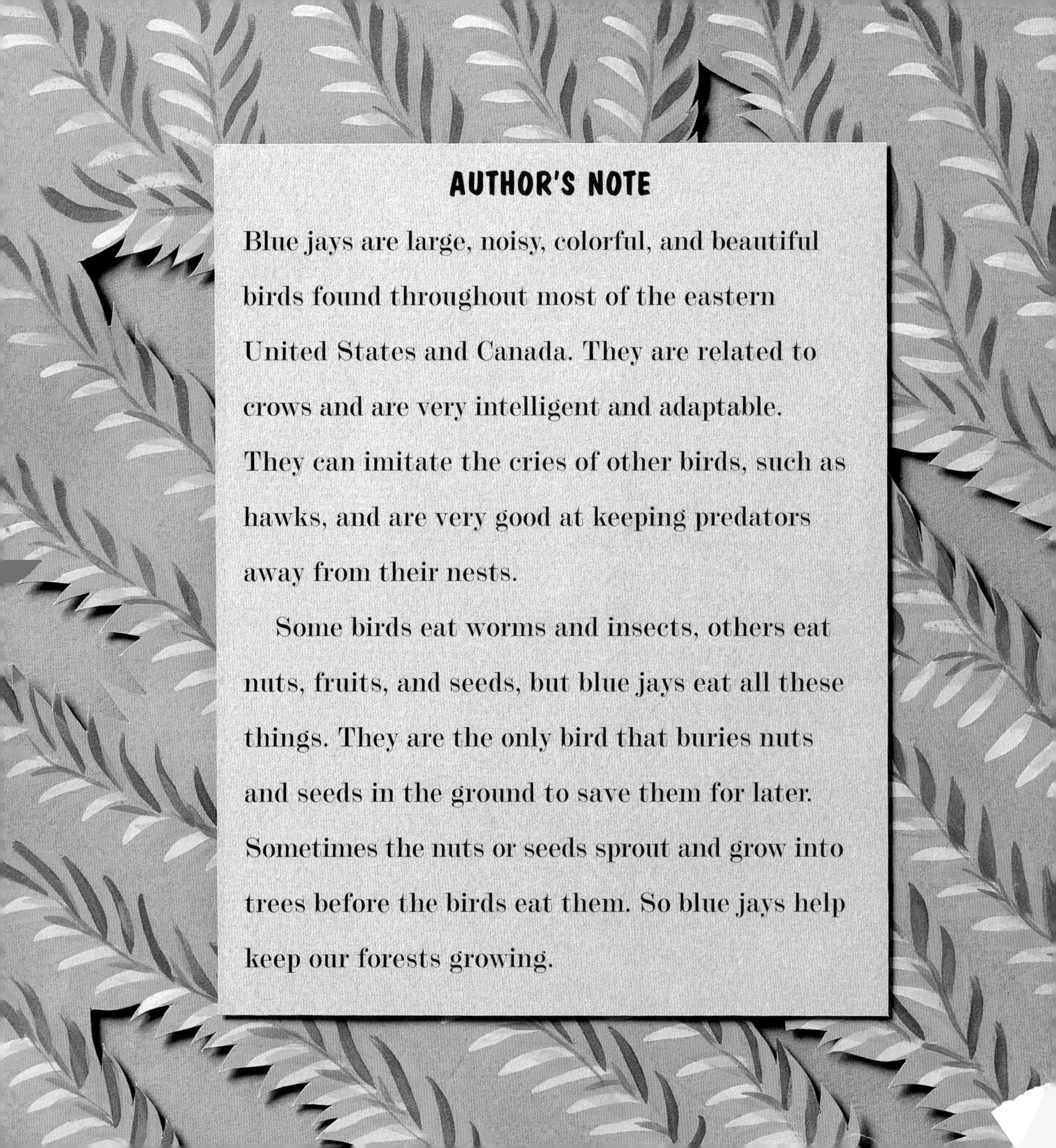

AUTHOR'S NOTE

Blue jays are large, noisy, colorful, and beautiful birds found throughout most of the eastern United States and Canada. They are related to crows and are very intelligent and adaptable. They can imitate the cries of other birds, such as hawks, and are very good at keeping predators away from their nests.

Some birds eat worms and insects, others eat nuts, fruits, and seeds, but blue jays eat all these things. They are the only bird that buries nuts and seeds in the ground to save them for later. Sometimes the nuts or seeds sprout and grow into trees before the birds eat them. So blue jays help keep our forests growing.

Cardinal
Chickadee
Mockingbird
Robin
Ruby-Throated
Hummingbird